About the Author

During his varied career, George has worked worldwide, especially in Africa with his wife, Liz, trotting alongside. Their three children and four grandchildren form a happy, close-knit family.

Short Bedtime Stories

George Stobbs

Short Bedtime Stories

Nightingale Books

A CIP catalogue record for this title is
available from the British Library.
ISBN 9781838750787

Nightingale Books is an imprint of
Pegasus Elliot MacKenzie Publishers Ltd.
www.pegasuspublishers.com

First Published in 2021

Nightingale Books
Sheraton House Castle Park
Cambridge England

Printed & Bound in Great Britain

Dedication

To Robbie and Joanna for whom
the stories were created.

Acknowledgements

To my dear supportive wife and to all of the others who provided constructive criticism.

Chapter 1
Enter the Goat

Imagine a small village high in the mountains, a few small fields and thick forest all around except where it overlooks a steep valley. Grey stone houses stand round the village green. There is a school, a blacksmith's forge, and a small shop. It is a very, very long way from anywhere else.

In the middle of the green stood a large white goat, thinking. A handsome animal, he had polished curly horns, a long white beard and, surprisingly, bright blue eyes. The goat had walked into the village a few minutes earlier and liked what he saw.

'Yes,' he thought, 'this is a good place for my wife and me to settle down.'

He watched the village children bouncing happily out of school, laughing and shouting to each other. There were twelve of them, aged between six and ten, dressed in long, well-worn trousers and home knitted jerseys of various colours.

The tallest child, who happened to be the eldest son of the village's mayor, was a lively, intelligent lad with a shock of red hair who was always smiling.

The smallest was a blonde girl with rosy cheeks and a runny nose. She held a length of string in one hand, the other end of which was tied round the neck of a large pink black - spotted pig.

The children ran over to the goat.

'I wonder where this animal came from?' said the mayor's son.

'I walked here,' said the goat.

The children backed away a little, slightly frightened. They had never heard of a goat that could talk.

'What's the pig's name?' asked the goat.

'Pig,' replied the little girl, 'and she's my best friend. What's your name?'

'Well,' said the goat, 'if your friend is Pig, you can call me Goat.'

By this time, a number of the villagers had gathered round. The mayor's wife, a large motherly lady with short, fair hair, shook her head.

'Goats don't talk,' she said.

'No,' replied Goat. 'My wife and I are magicians really, but we became very tired of people asking us to turn stones into gold (that's impossible, by the way), so we changed ourselves into other forms and walked away from the big city to find a peaceful life.'

'Nonsense. So where is this woman of yours?' asked the mayor's wife in a disbelieving tone of voice.

'Here,' replied Goat, looking behind him.

Out of the forest walked the most beautiful animal

the villagers had ever seen. Its coat was gleaming white, sparkling and shimmering in the sun. It looked a bit like a small horse but more delicate, a bit like a lady deer but stronger and not at all shy. But most of all, the villagers saw a single shining silver horn on its forehead. Everyone gasped.

'My wife,' said Goat, 'the beautiful Lady Unicorn.'

The mayor, a round, fussy little man, dressed in an old-fashioned black suit and with a large imitation gold chain round his neck, joined the group of villagers.

'Bah,' he exclaimed, shaking his head. 'Unicorns don't exist, it's just a horse with a bit of tin glued to its head.'

Lady Unicorn looked at him, bowed her head slightly, and walked up to him. He took two steps backward.

'Don't be afraid,' said Lady Unicorn. 'I won't hurt you.'

'Humph. This is all a trick. If you really are magicians, show us some magic.'

'You want to see some magic?' asked Goat. 'I don't suppose that you have many visitors here. Would you like to meet some new people?'

'Yes,' replied the mayor. 'It would be good to see some different faces.'

'Right,' said Goat. 'We could visit a village on the other side of the mountain.'

'Nonsense,' said the mayor. 'It would take at least a day to walk there.'

'Not by cloud tunnel,' laughed Goat.

Goat shook his head and tapped the ground twice with his right hoof. Above them, clouds began to swirl round and round, slowly forming a tunnel leading up and over the mountain behind the village. Goat tapped his hoof again, and the mouth of the tunnel came down, landing on the edge of the village green. It was a soft pink inside, and at the bottom was what looked like a thick red carpet with large bright orange circles.

'Step inside,' said the goat, 'and stand in the circles. Go on, it is perfectly safe.'

The mayor's wife, closely followed by her son and then the rest of the villagers, walked into the tunnel and stood on the orange circles. Last of all, the goat trotted in.

'All ready?' he asked.

'No,' said a small voice. 'Pig does not fit on a circle.'

Goat laughed and trotted over to Pig. Using his front legs, he quickly stretched a circle until it was Pig sized.

'Let's go,' he shouted. The circles began to move, slowly then faster, climbing up into the sky.

The villagers, a little frightened at first, began to enjoy the ride, the children squealing with excitement as the pink tunnel walls flashed by. After a few minutes, they began to go down until ahead of them they could see the mouth of the tunnel resting in the middle of a village very like their own.

They spilled out of the tunnel in excited groups. The villagers there were amazed to see them but soon got over their surprise. The mayor explained what had happened. In no time, a party was in full swing.

Several hours later, the mayor, full of party spirit, invited everyone back to his village.

'Maybe next week,' he said, 'you can come by cloud tunnel.'

So, back into the cloud tunnel they went and arrived home, tired and happy.

'You are very welcome to stay in our village. There's a nice dry barn that you and the Lady Unicorn could live in,' said the mayor to Goat.

'Thank you,' said Goat.

Lady Unicorn bowed her head. 'Yes, thank you,' she said, 'but I am a creature of the forest and will live there.'

'Goat, Goat, Goat,' chanted the children, running around him, stroking his nose (which he liked) and pulling his tail (which he did not). Then, everyone went off to bed, leaving Goat standing outside his barn, feeling very pleased with himself.

Chapter 2
The Troll

The troll lived in a big cave at the far side of the wood. He was big—as tall as three men standing on each other's heads. He was a sort of muddy green colour and had large yellowish teeth, bulging muscles, and huge, hairy hands. In fact, he looked a very scary monster indeed but was really a kind and generous creature. He was a vegetarian and did not eat children or goats. He had a beautiful garden in front of his cave where he grew potatoes, beans, carrots, and onions.

He loved to go out into the forest picking up large trees that had fallen down, taking them back to his cave where he carved fairies, goblins, pigs, dogs, or just strange shapes out of them. He had no tools, shaping the wood with his finger nails and polishing it with his horny hands.

Every few weeks, he would go down to the village, always at night, carrying a huge bucket in one hand and a gigantic basket in the other. He would go round the fields milking the cows. Once his bucket was full, he would then fill his basket with cow poo.

He loved cow poo and made great meals of it. Cow poo and carrots, cow poo and potatoes, cow poo sandwiches. But best of all, he would mix cow poo with the milk and make cow poo cheese, the smelliest, stinkiest cheese you could ever imagine.

In exchange, he always left presents for the villagers, usually a carving or two. The farmers complained because when they came to milk the cows the following morning, there was no milk left. But even though he had never hurt anyone, they were a little afraid of the troll—he was so big.

Ever since Goat had built the cloud corridor, the two villages often used it to meet for parties. At one party, the mayor of the Goat's village challenged the other village to a football match. This seemed a good idea at the time, but later, when they got back home, the villagers realised that they did not have a football pitch. There was a field which was big and flat enough, but it was littered with large boulders and several trees. The mayor asked Goat if he could use some of his magic to clear the field, but Goat said no. He thought that as the mayor had been silly enough to invite the other village, he should sort things out himself.

A few days later, Goat and his wife, the beautiful Lady Unicorn, were walking in the forest when they heard a horrible howling.

'Ouwwwwwww…ahhhhhooow,' on and on.

They trotted towards the noise and found the troll sitting outside his cave holding a swollen face and howling.

'He has toothache,' said Lady Unicorn. 'It's because of all that cow poo and him not brushing his teeth properly.'

She felt sorry for the troll, however, and trotted up to him. She touched his face gently with the tip of her horn and the troll was surrounded by a whirling mass of golden stars. His face began to glow, and the swelling disappeared.

'Wow, thank you,' said the troll. 'I feel so much better, and I promise to brush my teeth properly in the future. But, as you know, I always like to give something in return. What would you like?'

'Well,' said Lady Unicorn and explained about the football match.

'No problem,' said the troll. 'I'll fix it.'

The next day, the troll came down to the village. He walked into the field and pulled out the trees, putting them carefully to one side so that they could be planted again. He lifted the rocks, piling them into a big mound where pretty flowers could be planted. Then, he walked over the field flattening it with his huge, horny feet. Finally, he went back to his cave and came back with six nicely carved lengths of wood which he put together to make goal posts.

Everyone was very happy, and the mayor thanked the troll, giving him a large bag of cow poo from his own special cows.

A week later, the football match took place (the score was twenty each because none of the villagers were very good at football), and the troll was the guest of honour, but only after he'd brushed his teeth to get rid of the cow poo smell.

Chapter 3
The Star Ship

Goat and the beautiful Lady Unicorn were standing at the edge of the forest looking up at the silky black night sky.

'Look at all those stars,' said Lady Unicorn.

'I wish I could fly through space and see a thousand different worlds,' replied Goat.

As they talked, they could see a bright light falling fast out of the sky.

'Look out!' shouted Goat. 'It's coming towards us.'

They ran back into the forest and, with a deafening swoosh, something flew past and landed with a loud crash among the trees near them.

Goat shook his head, half deafened by the noise.

'Let's go and see,' he said, and they trotted off quickly through the trees.

In a few minutes, they found a large silver disc, slightly battered, lying among a great pile of flattened bushes and broken tree branches.

'I wonder if there is anyone inside, and, if there is, I hope that they have not been hurt,' said Lady

Unicorn. 'Is there a door into that thing?'

'Yes,' replied Goat. 'Look, it seems to be slightly open, but I don't see anyone. We can't help as we are. We'd better get back to human form, then try to open the door.'

Goat tapped his left hoof on the ground while the beautiful Lady Unicorn waved her horn and, with a twinkling of gold stars, they changed back into humans. As animals, they wore no clothes, so they quickly got dressed (they always carried some with them, just in case). Goat became a tall man with long fingers, twinkling eyes, and a fine, black beard. The Lady Unicorn was slim and neat with short, dark hair.

They walked up to the door of the silver disc.

'Careful,' said Goat. 'Let me go first.'

He pulled at the door, but it did not move. He pushed it, then pulled it again.

'No good, it won't open.'

Lady Unicorn sniffed and leaned forward, pressing a little green button on one side of the door. As it opened, she looked at Goat. 'Call yourself a magician,' she said.

Inside, the disc was lit with a pale blue light. Goat and Lady Unicorn carefully stepped inside.

'Smells of peppermint,' said Goat.

'And chocolate,' Lady Unicorn added. 'Interesting.'

They walked along a short corridor until they came to a round door which glowed pink and white and, like the outside door, had a small, green button on one side. Goat pressed it and, with a gentle hiss, the door opened. Inside was a large room lined with shelves filled with shiny jars, all neatly labelled. There were two metal desks and lots of gleaming metal cupboards.

'Goodness,' said Goat. 'This is so clean, it hurts your eyes to look at it.'

At the far end of the room was another door. As they neared it, it opened automatically, and they walked through into a control room with large circular windows all round. On one side was a large desk with lots of levers and flashing lights. Two creatures were slumped over it. They looked a little like octopuses, with large pale pink heads and lots of arms. Lady Unicorn ran over to them.

'They are alive,' she said. She stroked them gently, but nothing happened.

'Let me help,' said Goat, and he placed his long fingers over her shorter ones.

Together, they stroked the strange creatures and golden stars began to float around them as the magic worked. Slowly the creatures began to stir. They opened their huge violet-blue eyes and began to make gabbling noises when they saw Goat and Lady Unicorn.

'Don't be afraid,' she said to them. The creatures looked at each other. One reached into a cupboard and put on a small blue, sparkling hat.

'Now I have my communicator on,' said the creature. 'Who are you?'

The Lady Unicorn explained.

'But', she asked, 'who are you and where are you from?'

'We are from another world a very long way from here,' the creature replied. 'We are here on an important mission. We have come to find new tastes as everything on our planet tastes like broccoli. We have lots of different sorts of fruit: big red ones, small pink ones, green long ones, white curly ones, purple, black and orange berries, but they all taste the same, broccoli, broccoli, broccoli. We have found so many wonderful tastes on your planet and have stored them. Orange, mint, strawberry, and, best of all, chocolate. When we get back home, we will make the most wonderful sweets. Unfortunately, we have run out of fuel and don't know how we will get there.'

'What sort of fuel do you need?' asked Goat.

'Eggs,' replied the creature. 'Maybe six of them.'

'Eggs?' Goat was very surprised.

'Yes,' replied the creature. 'Our engine eats eggs and turns them into pure energy. Six will get us back home.'

'No problem,' said Goat.

He walked off to the village and came back an hour later with six eggs. The creature opened a small cover in the control desk and pushed the eggs in, one by one. As each one disappeared in, the machine gave a loud, satisfied burp.

'Excellent, the engine is happy and fully fuelled. Would you like to come with us and see our world?'

'Thanks,' said Goat, 'but no. We are happy here.'

They all said goodbye. Goat and Lady Unicorn climbed back out of the entrance door, closing it behind them. The spaceship made a whirring noise and began to climb slowly. When it reached tree-top height, there was a loud swoosh, and it soared upwards into the night sky.

'I thought you wanted to see other worlds,' said Lady Unicorn.

'Yes,' replied Goat, 'but I can't stand broccoli.'

Chapter 4
Silver Tiger

The village children sat on the summer grass. Goat stood happily under his favourite tree.

'I'll tell you a story,' said Goat. 'Have you ever watched a bubbling river laughing in the sunlight, and seen a sudden silver light in the water? Or perhaps walking through a wood or down a forest path, you have seen a silver flash out of the corner of your eye? Perhaps you have just seen a silver tiger. Silver tigers do not glow, they shimmer. They have sleek, bright silver coats with black tiger stripes, bright blue eyes, and large, furry paws. They are magical animals and can change colour to blend in with their surroundings, making themselves almost invisible. This is why you almost never see a silver tiger.

'In a big city, down at the coast, there was a large company called Megacoat, which made and sold clothes. These were made by very poorly paid people, often children, who had to work long hours cutting cloth and sewing it together. The clothes that the company sold were no better than those made by other companies, but cleverly, they gave clothes to the king, so that they could tell everyone that the king wore their clothes. Everyone wanted to be like the king, so they bought Megacoat's jackets, dresses, and pants, but most of all, their coats. All the fashionable ladies wore them.

'One day, the king called the boss of the company to the palace and told him that the queen wanted a coat made of silver tiger fur. "And", he said, "I want this within a month, or in future I will only wear clothes made by Grandee Garments, your big rival".

'Once back at his factory, the boss spoke with his best coat makers who told him that they would need the fur from three silver tigers to make the coat. "Ok", thought the boss, "but I will need a lot more than that because once people see the queen wearing the coat, everyone will want one".

'He called in a famous hunter and said that he wanted the skins from five hundred silver tigers. "That will be difficult", advised the hunter, "but not impossible". The boss promised him a lot of money for every tiger skin that he brought in.

'How do you catch a silver tiger? The hunter knew a way. Silver Tigers love cream cakes, especially chocolate cream cakes. He bought six very chocolatey cakes with cream spilling out from their middles and set off into the forest. He found a place under a big tree, then made a big noose in a long rope he carried, passing one end over a branch of the tree. Carefully he placed the noose in a circle on the ground. Then he put the biggest, creamiest cake down in the middle of the noose. Taking the other end of the rope in his hands, he hid behind a big bush and waited. He waited a long time, but hunters are very patient people.

'After several hours, he saw a flash of silver and a beautiful silver tigress walked slowly up to the cake. It licked its lips and bent down to take a bite. The hunter pulled hard on the end of the rope and the noose tightened around the tigress' neck. She growled and pulled on the rope, jumping up and down, but the hunter held on. Eventually the tigress stopped moving and the hunter, tying the end of the rope to a tree, pulled out a big knife and walked up to her. "Well tiger", he said, "I want your coat".

'The tigress looked at him with her ice blue eyes. "You mean to kill me", she said.

'"Of course", said the hunter, "and another five hundred or so of your kind".

'"Well", said the tigress, "I do not want to be killed, so if you let me go, I will bring many tigers to your trap. Then you will have five hundred within a few weeks, otherwise it will take you years".

'"How do I know that you will not just run away"? asked the hunter.

'"I will leave you my most treasured possession", replied the tigress. "Take the silver chain from around my neck". The hunter looked and, sure enough, there was a heavy silver chain with a strangely carved pendant on it, and in the centre of the pendant was a glowing red jewel.

'The hunter took it off her neck. The jewel flashed and at once, the chain wrapped itself round his wrists, tying them together.

'"Now, I have caught you", said the tigress. "Tell me why you want 500 tiger skins".

'The hunter then told her the story of the queen's coat and Megacoat's plan to make lots of tiger skin coats.

'"But", said the tigress, very shocked, "that would kill every tiger in the land. Megacoat must be taught a lesson".

'"Let me go", said the hunter, "and I will take you to the big boss' house".

'The tigress blinked her ice-blue eyes, and the chain around the hunter's wrists wrapped itself round his neck. "So long as you do what you are told, the chain will not hurt you. I will leave you now, but I will be back in a few hours with some of my friends".

'As soon as she had gone, the hunter started to run off, but had only gone a few steps before the chain around his neck began to tighten. He stopped and took a step back. At once the chain loosened a little. He realised that he could not run away.

'A few hours later, the tigress returned with another twenty-nine silver tigers, all shimmering in the sunlight and staring at him with ice-blue eyes.

'"Take us to the man who thought of this evil plan", they growled. The hunter had no choice but to agree.

'They reached the city just as night was falling and suddenly, the tigers seemed to disappear as they changed colour to match their surroundings.

'Eventually, they reached a large house. The hunter banged on the door and the Megacoat boss came to the door.

'"I've brought you 30 tigers", said the hunter.

'At that, the tigers changed into shimmering silver again and surrounded the boss. "You wanted to kill us all. Now, take us to the king", they demanded.

'The Megacoat boss was very frightened. "The king will kill me. Please let me go".

"At least he will not cut your skin off", said the tigers. "Take us to the palace".

'So, the Megacoat boss, the hunter, and thirty tigers set off to the palace, the tigers changing colour so they could not be seen.

'The palace guards knew the Megacoat boss well, so they let him in, taking everyone (although they did not see the tigers) to the great hall where the king and queen were waiting.

'"So", said the king. "Where are the silver tigers"?

'"Here we are", they replied, becoming shimmering silver once more.

'The king was about to call his guards when the lady tigress that had caught the hunter spoke.

'"Before you call the guards, let us speak. Your kingdom is very beautiful, but it is not rich. What you need is a lot of visitors who will spend a lot of money here. A wise and noble monarch like yourself can easily see that to do this, you need something that no one else has: silver tigers. All you have to do is make a law stopping all hunting in the forest, then start up a tourist company. You could call it Royal Silver Tiger Tours. One or two of us would always be around shimmering silver for the tourists to photograph".

'"Wait a minute", said the hunter, "What about me? If all hunting is stopped, I won't have a job".

'"Don't be silly", said the tigress, "You know the forest better than anyone. You would be the head tour guide".

"What about me?" asked the Megacoat boss.

'The tigress looked at him with her ice-blue eyes. "You tried to kill all the silver tigers," she said, "and, if you had done that, the king would not have been able to make his wonderful wildlife park. He, in his royal wisdom, should decide what should be done with you."

(The king, of course, was the one who had wanted a tiger skin coat for the queen, but he had forgotten that and now thought that the whole tourist idea was his .)

'"Harrumph," said the king. (He often harrumphed because he thought that it made him sound important.) "He should be made to work twelve hours a day in his own factory, making coats for his badly paid workers.

'In a few months, it was all done. Flocks of tourists

came to see the silver tigers and the king became rich. So did many others in the kingdom. Restaurants and hotels were opened, farmers sold their meat, fruit, and vegetables to the hotels. Weavers wove colourful scarves and woolly hats which the tourists bought. The hunter came to love the animals of the forest and helped them whenever he could. And the silver tigers shimmered through the trees, as they had promised.'

Goat stretched happily in the sunshine and quietly scratched his bottom on a tree. 'Home with you,' he told the children. 'So, next time you see a silver flash out of the corner of your eye, it might just be a silver tiger, but don't be afraid, it will only want a cream cake.'

Chapter 5
The Haunted House

The mayor's son (known as T because his real name was very long) was always getting into trouble. He loved adventures and would climb trees, jump into rivers, or would get lost in the forest. He was often late back home, usually with torn and dirty clothes. One day he came home with no bottom on his trousers because he had been sliding down a big rock. His parents always forgave him because he was very good humoured with a big smile, always told the truth, and enjoyed life so much.

His younger sister (known as Ttoo) adored him and followed him from adventure to adventure with Pig happily trotting along beside her. She was much more careful than her brother and generally came home a lot cleaner than he did. They were great friends with the blacksmith's three children, two girls (twins called Silver and Gold) and a boy, ten years old, called Rock.

Just outside the village, on the edge of the forest, was a tumble-down old house. Part of the thatched roof was missing; the windows were broken and the doors swung loose when the wind blew. The garden was very overgrown, and several large trees bent over the house, making it dark and spooky. Because they thought that their children might hurt themselves, the village parents ordered their children not to go inside. The village children thought that it was probably haunted and most stayed well away.

'Let's go and explore the haunted house,' said T, a big grin on his face. 'If there is a ghost there, it is bound to come out tonight as it is Halloween. We'll set off just before it gets dark.'

The blacksmith's children agreed, but Ttoo suggested that they ask Goat to come along 'Just in case.'

Late that afternoon, the five children, a happy snuffling Pig, and an amused Goat set off. Arriving at the house, they looked through the windows but could not see much as they were cracked and dirty with spiders' webs all over them. They walked up to the front door. T pushed and it slowly creaked open.

They walked into the front room. It was empty except for a table in the middle and an old, cracked mirror on one wall. At the far end was a closed, green door, the paint peeling off. There was a loud creak, and they all jumped.

'Maybe it's the ghost,' said Ttoo.

Her brother laughed. 'There's no ghost.'

He walked towards the door and, just as he was about to open it, a hand came through the wood, followed by an arm, a leg, and finally, a little old man, dressed in an old-fashioned black coat and yellow waistcoat, stood in front of them. He looked very tired, very sad, and not quite solid.

The children ran towards the front door, but Goat did not move. 'Don't be afraid,' he told them.

'Good evening,' he said to the ghost, who looked at him with unhappy eyes. 'Why are you here?'

The old man coughed and explained in a very hoarse voice, 'I live here. I lived here for more than fifty years with my wife and children, but my wife fell ill and died, my children went away to work in the big city, so I was left on my own. At first, I would have visits from other people in the village, but I sent them away, telling them that I just wanted to be on my own, so they stopped coming.

'Then, one morning, I got out of bed and found that I was floating and could walk through walls. I realised that I had become a ghost. I did not need to eat or sleep. I have been like that for years. It is terribly, terribly boring. I tried to talk to the few people who came near the house, but they ran away, scared of me. I would not hurt them. I could not, even if I wanted to. So, I became very, very lonely.'

'Do you have to be in this house?' asked Silver.

'No,' replied the ghost, 'but I have nowhere else to go and I do not want to frighten people.' He looked miserable, and a tear ran down his face.

The children felt very sorry for him.

'Do you like donkeys?' asked Goat.

The ghost thought for a moment. 'I suppose so,' he replied. 'Why do you ask?'

'You could come and live with me in my barn, which I share with two donkeys. They are nice, friendly animals. You would have some company.'

'We would come and visit,' said the children, jumping up and down with excitement. What fun it would be to have a ghost as a friend.

'If you did not like it,' said Goat, 'you could always come back here.'

The ghost began to smile—a shy little smile which he had not used for years. 'I think that I would like that very much,' he said, and the children cheered.

So the ghost, whose name was Henry, came to live in the barn with Goat and the two donkeys. He was still sad sometimes, but when the children came to visit, he would smile his shy smile and walk through the barn walls just because he could.

Chapter 6
The Golden Dragon

Goat stood in the barn surrounded by the village children. It was raining hard. 'Please tell us a story… about a dragon,' said Gold, the blacksmith's daughter. The children sat down on some bales of hay and looked expectantly at Goat.

'In a cave in the middle of a dark forest,' he began, 'lived a dragon. She was very large, with glowing red eyes and shining golden scales. Strangely, for a dragon, she was vegetarian and did not eat thousands of sheep or, for that matter, children.

'One day she woke up to a terrible noise and found lots of men cutting down trees near her cave. Other men were levelling the ground, ready to build a big factory. When the men saw her, they threw away their picks and shovels and ran. She was horrified. She couldn't stay, but where would she go?

'She spread her great golden wings and took to the air, flying higher and higher. After a while, she saw, far below, a large green meadow with a gentle river running through it. "I could live there", she thought and glided down. As she landed however, she was

met by a large herd of very angry cows bellowing and pointing their horns at her. "Oh dear", she thought, "they think that I've come to eat them. I can't stay here". Up and up she flew. It was wintertime, and in the distance, she could see some snowy mountains. Thinking that she might find a nice, peaceful cave there, she flew towards them.

'When she got there, she found that the mountains were barren and rocky, and there were no nice caves to be seen. She had flown a long way and was very tired. Eventually, she saw a small village. It looked very poor. The houses seemed to be almost falling down, the thatched roofs tattered, and there was no smoke from the chimneys although it was very cold.

'She landed in a small field, happy to have a rest. Looking around, she saw a little girl walking across the field towards her. She looked very cold and had no warm clothes. Seeing the dragon she stopped. "Wow", she said, "you are very beautiful".

'"Thank you", replied the dragon, "and you look very cold".

'"I am. We are very poor and have no money for warm clothes. Also, a few years ago a bad disease killed all of the trees, so we have no wood to burn. It is cold outside, but even colder in our house".

'The dragon breathed on her, a gentle warm breath.

'"Oh, that's lovely", said the girl. "Can I go and bring back my brother? He's also cold".

41

'"Of course", replied the dragon. A few minutes later, each child was standing in front of her, both warm.

'"Mum and Dad are cold too", said the boy.

'"So is everyone else, I suppose", replied the dragon.

'The children led the dragon into the village. She was very careful not to knock anything over as the road was narrow. They reached the children's house and their parents rushed out terrified that the dragon would eat everyone. The girl explained that the dragon was a friend and would not do any harm. The dragon then put its nose through the front door and puffed in warm air. Soon the neighbours gathered round and the dragon went from house to house, warming the whole village.

'When spring came, the dragon told everyone that she was going away to find a comfortable cave.

'"No, no", shouted the villagers. "Please stay with us". The dragon was very pleased and settled down in a large barn.

'Over the next few months, the story of the dragon that had warmed the village spread throughout the land and people began to arrive to see the wonderful dragon for themselves. The village was a long way from anywhere else, so these people needed somewhere to stay. At first the villagers took them into their houses, charging them a small amount for bed and breakfast. Later, they built a small hotel with the money that they had earned. There was then room for more visitors, and a tea room opened.

'The village blacksmith began to make small models of the dragon to sell, and the women of the village made dragon pies and delicious dragon fudge. There was soon enough money to mend the houses and to plant trees. The dragon lived happily among friends, and no one was cold any more.'

Printed in Great Britain
by Amazon

79705216R10025